Amber's
Dressing Up
Dreams

The Glass
Slippers

LOOK OUT FOR MORE OF

The Satin Dress
The Diamond Tiara
The Velvet Cloak
The Glass Slippers

COMING SOON

Lily's Dressing-up Dreams
The Silver Mirror
The Flowered Apron
The Pearly Comb
The Lace Gown

Pearl's Dressing-up Dreams

Amber's Dressing-Up Dreams

The Glass Slippers

JENNY OLDFIELD

Hodder
Children's
Books

A division of Hachette Children's Books

A Catalogue record for this book is available from the British Library

ISBN-13: 978 0 340 95596 3

Printed and bound in Great Britain
by Clays Ltd, St Ives plc

The paper and board used in this paperback by Hodder Children's
Books are natural recyclable products made from wood grown
insustainable forests. The manufacturing processes conform to the
environmental regulations of the country of origin.

Hodder Children's Books
A division of Hachette Children's Books
338 Euston Rd, London NW1 3BH
An Hachette Livre UK company

Pearl and Lily had stayed away from Amber's house for a whole week.

"Amber is talking rubbish!" Lily said.

"Yes," Pearl agreed. "All that stuff about her fairy godmother waving a magic wand! It can't be true!"

Today the girls were hanging about outside Amber's gate. "Definitely a big fib," Lily muttered.

"Hi, Pearl. Hi, Lily." Amber popped out from behind the hedge. "Long time no see!"

"Erm, yeah," Lily stammered.

"We've been – er – busy," Pearl said.

"It's OK, I know you didn't believe me when I told you about Cinderella world. It sounded mad, even to me. So I don't blame you for avoiding me."

"You don't?" Pearl and Lily said.

"No way." She watched the frowns on her friends' faces melt away. ". . . But it's still true!"

Back came the frowns. "You're crazy," Pearl muttered.

"Totally nuts," Lily agreed. "No way can anybody step into a fairy tale."

"Not just by dressing up in some old

clothes." Pearl sounded certain.

"If you don't believe me, why don't you come and see?" Amber said brightly.

Lily and Pearl backed away until Amber grabbed their hands and pulled them towards the house.

"Come on – I dare you!" she said.

"This is where the magic happens," Amber explained. She opened her dressing-up box and started to pull things out. There was a red and yellow clown costume, a blue plastic builder's helmet, a Mickey Mouse mask and a pair of tottery party shoes belonging to Amber's mum.

"So if I put this on, magic happens?" Lily checked as she picked up the orange clown wig.

"It doesn't work with everything in the box," Amber told her. "But try it on and see."

"No, it's too smelly." Lily threw the wig back in the box.

"Scaredy cat!" Pearl picked up the wig and perched it on top of her auburn curls. She twirled on the spot. "See – nothing happened!"

"Huh!" Lily grunted.

"Try this." Amber offered Lily a blue silk shawl with a long fringe.

The shawl came down to Lily's feet. The fringe tripped her up when she attempted a twirl.

"Huh!" Pearl gave a disgusted cough. She tried on the builder's helmet and the mouse mask both together. "Wrraaagh!"

she said in a scary voice.

Lily laughed as she stepped into the baggy clown trousers. "Come on, Amber, admit it. You've been kidding us about this magic stuff. It's a big fat fib!"

Now Amber was cross. "It's so not a fib!" she insisted. "And it's not funny either, Lily! Not when you're Cinderella and you're sitting in some dark, dingy cellar and a man in a black cloak is trying to kidnap you and the Uglies are hitting you and pinching you and turning you black and blue!"

"Wow!" Lily stared at Amber.

"She definitely means it," Pearl said under her breath.

"Hey, come on, Amber, don't sulk," Lily coaxed. "We didn't mean to upset you."

"Yes you did," Amber grumbled, shoving her feet into her mum's old party shoes. "But I don't care – you can think what you like. I know that my dressing-up box is magic. Just you wait and see!"

Lily and Pearl watched Amber totter across the basement in her high heels.

Wobble-wobble – she reached the bottom of the stairs.

The shoes were covered in gold and silver sequins which twinkled in the light.

"Watch it, Amber, you'll sprain your ankle!" Lily warned.

Amber turned and staggered. She lost her balance and turned again as a brilliant white light appeared.

"Where did that come from?" Pearl asked, backing into a corner.

Lily shielded her eyes from the dazzling light. "Oh no!" she muttered under her breath.

The light grew brighter still. Amber turned in her party shoes which glittered gold and silver.

"Is it happening?" Pearl gasped. "Amber, stop spinning. Tell us if this is what you meant!"

But Amber knew it was too late. The shoes were magic. They were spinning her off into Cinderella world where Lily and Pearl couldn't follow.

"Amber, we believe you!" the two girls cried. "We're sorry we've been horrid. Amber, come back!"

There was a big orange pumpkin on the table in the Cinderella cellar. Amber arrived in a silver and gold cloud which lit up the dark room. She flipped off her magic party shoes then spotted six white sugar-mice sitting beside the pumpkin.

"So this turns into the coach and horses to take me to the party!" she groaned.

"Ah, Cinderella, there you are, my

dear." The fairy godmother fluttered down the chimney and landed daintily on the table. "I've been looking everywhere for you!"

"Sorry, I've been busy," Amber muttered, glancing down and seeing that she was in her Cinderella rags.

"I bought the pumpkin from the market and the six sugar-mice were in the cupboard over there," Fairy G explained, shaking soot from her shimmering wings. "But we're in such a rush. The ball is about to begin and you're not even dressed!"

"Never mind. Let's forget it," Amber said. "I've told you before – dancing with soppy old Prince Charming is the last thing I want to do!"

Fairy G laughed with a high, tinkling sound. "Don't be silly, dear. Every girl in the kingdom wants to dance with the Prince. He's so handsome and . . . rich!"

Rich is good, Amber thought. She pictured the film stars and footballers in the celebrity mags back home. *And handsome is OK, I suppose.*

Then she quickly put a stop to her wandering thoughts. *Whoa! Get real, Amber! This is a fairy tale, remember. This is not where you belong!*

"I still don't want to go," Amber insisted. She picked up one of the sugar-mice which Buttons had brought her when she first landed here. "Can't you understand that you're wasting your time?"

"Nonsense!" the fairy laughed. She

tapped her wand against the table. "Now where will I find two green lizards?"

"Lizards?" Amber echoed.

"Coachmen, dear, coachmen!" The tinkling laugh couldn't hide the fact that Fairy G was irritated. "Come now, Cinderella, it's not like you to be so dim."

Ah yes, coachmen. A golden coach, six white horses and two coachmen in green velvet uniforms. "Maybe we could do without the coachmen?" Amber suggested.

But her fairy godmother tutted and flew off up the chimney. "I'll search the hill above the Prince's Palace!" she said as she vanished.

Which left Amber to sit by the dying embers of the fire and think.

17

It's quiet down here, she said to herself. *Spookily quiet!*

Of course – the house would be empty now except for her doddery dad. The Uglies and Octavia would already have set off for the ball.

Maybe they left the cellar door unlocked! The sudden thought made her jump up and race up the cellar steps. She turned the door handle. *No, they locked it to make sure I couldn't get out. Silly me to think they'd forget!*

So glumly she went down again and made her next plan.

I could gobble down the sugar-mice then there'd be no horses to pull the coach. Or else I could climb the chimney and run away! she thought. Anything to get out of dancing

18

with the Prince and everything that happened after. *I've been up that chimney before, so why not again?*

Amber peered up the wide chimney which got narrower towards the top. It ended in a little round patch of daylight, high above the street.

"Pppffffhhhh!" she spluttered as black soot showered over her face.

Her fairy godmother was back, floating down the chimney, scattering soot as her wings brushed the sides.

It was too late to escape.

"Two lizards from a sunny rock on the hill!" the fairy announced, releasing the small, scaly creatures to scuttle across the table.

"Poor things," Amber murmured.

"Stand back!" her godmother ordered, preparing to wave her wand and perform great magic.

"B-b-but!" Amber protested.

"No buts, dear." The fairy sighed and drew herself up tall. "Listen to me, Cinderella – I've gone to an awful lot of trouble to make things nice for you, and this is the thanks I get!" She wagged her tiny finger over Amber's ingratitude. "I find you the most beautiful pink satin gown and blue velvet cloak and the most precious diamond and ruby tiara which every other girl would die for!"

"I know," Amber muttered with an embarrassed frown.

Agitated, her fairy godmother fluttered around the cellar, alighting on the table at last. "And when you disappear without warning, even then I carry on with my plans. I buy a big, juicy pumpkin from the market. I search the entire house until I find the six sugar-mice."

"Which Buttons gave me as a present," Amber pointed out. *I should have gobbled them down all in one go!* she thought sourly.

"Buttons is a nice boy," the fairy agreed. "Don't frown, Cinderella. It will give you wrinkles. In any case, we're wasting time talking. Let's get on."

"B-b-but!"

Fairy G rose from the table and flew right up to Amber's face.

Flutter-flutter. Amber felt the breeze from her wings.

"NO MORE BUTS!" the fairy roared in a fierce voice. "There's no use complaining and going into a sulk, Cinderella, for I have made up my mind and you *shall* go to the ball!"

Whoosh! Cinderella's fairy godmother wafted her wand over the orange pumpkin, and – *pop!* – a gorgeous golden coach appeared. They were out of the cellar, in the wide street in front of the grand house.

Whoosh-whoosh-whoosh! Whoosh-whoosh . . . Whoosh! The wand swished over the sugar-mice, and – *whoa!* – six magnificent white horses stood ready to pull the coach.

Amber gasped. She'd never seen anything so beautiful.

Next the fairy passed her wand over the lizards. *Whoosh-whoosh!* Up sprang two smart coachmen in green uniforms with gold braid, wearing white wigs tied into neat ponytails.

"I wish Pearl and Lily were here," Amber said out loud. "Then they'd *have* to believe me!"

"Almost ready," the fairy promised.

One of the coachmen held open the coach door. The other sat up in the driving seat.

Fairy G was still dishing out the orders. "Stand still, Cinderella, while I get you dressed."

More *whooshes* with the wand.

Amber gazed down at her smooth pink satin gown with its pink ribbons and

25

creamy pearls embroidered down the front. She touched the soft blue velvet cloak with her fingertips and felt the tiny diamonds encrusted in the high collar.

Whoosh! Still more action with the wand, then Amber looked in the coach window and saw her reflection, complete with the precious diamond and ruby tiara.

"Lovely!" the fairy sighed. But then she glanced down at Amber's bare feet and went into a tizz. "No shoes!" she gasped. "Oh my! Oh dear! Cinderella, you can't go barefoot to the ball!"

"That's it then – it's all off!" Amber was still looking for a way out. The coach could turn back into a pumpkin, the horses into mice and the coachmen into lizards for all she cared.

"Stand still!" the fairy said in her fierce voice.

Fidgety Amber froze on the spot.

A big *whoosh!* Amber looked down at her feet to see a sparkling, shimmering pair of glass shoes.

When they say glass, they mean lots and lots of tiny glass crystals, she thought. *Because of course if they were made of solid glass they'd crack and break. Or else, they'd be too stiff to walk in, so it wouldn't make sense!*

No – these wondrous glass slippers were made of thousands of cut glass crystals sewn on to white satin, with tiny slim heels and little pink bows to match her dress.

"Perfect!" her fairy godmother said. "You're ready at last. Cinderella, your coach awaits you!"

"Thanks," Amber muttered. The little word didn't sound big enough, considering the effort the crotchety fairy had put in.

Just then, as Amber stepped into the golden coach, the front door opened and Cinderella's dad stepped out. "Oh!" he said in amazement, peering with short-sighted eyes through his gold-rimmed glasses. "Cinderella, my dear, is that you?"

"Yes, it's me." She scowled at Tom the footman who stood on duty by the door. *And you can wipe that smirk off your face!* she thought.

"But, my dear girl, you look like a . . . like a princess!" the old man stammered. "So pretty in your ball gown, with your hair so shiny, like a blackbird's wing . . . Yes, every inch a princess!"

Amber's heart softened at the old man's happiness. She gave him a warm smile.

"Thank you," she murmured. And she meant it.

"Hurry now," Cinderella's proud dad told the coachman. He took off his glasses and wiped away tears of joy. "Take my daughter to the Prince's Palace before the Ball begins!"

And so they were off down the street, the white horses prancing as the coachman

cracked his whip. Their silver bridles jingled, the wheels rumbled forward and Cinderella waved goodbye.

"Oh my! Oh my! I almost forgot." The fairy godmother was in a tizz again. She sped after the coach, light as a feather, leaving a trail of silver and gold glitter behind her.

"What now?" Amber glanced sideways

to see the fairy tapping hard at the window. She opened it and leaned out.

"Before you go, I have something important to tell you," Fairy G gabbled. "It is this, Cinderella. When you arrive at the Prince's Palace you will be the prettiest girl there. Everyone will admire you and you will be the centre of attention."

Amber cringed back into the coach. *Nightmare – I'm not the showy-offy kind!* she thought.

"But," the fairy went on, tapping her wand sternly against the window, "there is one thing you must remember!"

"Oh yeah, the stuff about being back by midnight," Amber cut in. "Don't worry, I know all that."

"Don't interrupt!" Fairy G scolded. "You

will have a wonderful time at the Ball and you will be the envy of everyone there. But when the fireworks begin and the clock strikes twelve, you must leave the Palace and come home to your father."

"That's what I said!" Amber pointed out. "Anyway, being a party pooper and leaving early is no problem. If it was down to me, I wouldn't be going at all, remember!"

But the fairy gave her that familiar don't-argue-with-me look.

"OK, OK!" Amber gave in. "I'll be back by midnight. Coachman, drive on!"

4

The lamplit streets were almost deserted. Everyone was already at the Palace, waiting for the Ball to begin.

Clip-clop went the horses' hooves on the hard cobbles. Inside the coach, Amber hung on as they rode over bumps and round corners towards the bottom of the hill where the Prince's house stood.

Looking glumly out of the window,

Amber saw a stray cat slink across the road and away into the shadows, and a boy in a buttoned-up jacket sitting by the town fountain, whittling at a piece of wood.

"'This little piggy went to mar-ket!'" he chanted as he worked away at the stick and chips of wood flew off at all angles. "'This little piggy stayed at home . . .'"

Amber recognised the boy, asked the coachman to stop the coach then flung open the window. "Buttons!" she yelled across the square.

He sprang up, knife and stick in hand. "What are you staring at me for?" he called back. "I ain't done nothing!"

"Buttons, it's me – Amb — er, Cinderella! Don't you recognise me?"

Her old friend and ally came closer and

35

peered into the coach. "Blimey!" he muttered, blowing out his cheeks and letting the air escape with a loud "Puhhh!"

"Stop staring at me like I was an alien!" Amber wrinkled her nose. "It's only me – Cinders!"

"Are you sure?" Buttons shook his head. "You've got the same colour hair as Cinderella, and the same wide, frog-mouth . . ."

"My mouth isn't like a frog's!" she protested.

". . . The same twinkly brown eyes," he went on doubtfully. "But look at the pearls and lace, the diamonds and ribbons. Whoa, Cinders – what happened?"

"It's a long story," Amber muttered.

"Anyway, what are you doing here? Why aren't you up at the Palace?"

Buttons shrugged. "I don't like parties."

"Me neither. But I've been forced to go."

Climbing on to the step of the golden coach, Buttons took a peek inside at the plush red velvet cushions. "Blimey!" he said again. "But listen, Cinders, the Uglies and my lady Octavia ain't going to be happy when you show up."

"No need to tell me," she agreed. "Actually, I'm dreading the next bit."

"Where you walk in and all the boys go 'Wow!' and the girls turn up their snooty noses?" he asked with a cheeky grin.

Amber nodded and sighed. "Buttons, why don't you come with me?"

But he jumped down to the ground. "Sorry, Cinders, it's not for me."

"It could be," she argued. "The Prince invited the whole town . . ."

"Watch my lips. N-O – no!" he said. Then, looking up at the coachman, he told him to crack his whip and get on his way.

The horses took the strain and eased the coach forward.

"B-b-but!" Amber cried, leaning out of

the window to watch her friend's disappearing figure.

"Bye, Cinders!" Buttons called, going back to his perch at the edge of the fountain. "'This little piggy had roast beef . . .'" He carved the stick with his knife. "'And this little piggy had none . . .'"

Soon the coach stopped at the steps leading to Prince Charming's Palace. The coachman at the back of the carriage jumped down and held open Amber's door.

Amber stepped down. The hem of her pink satin gown floated just above the ground, her little glass slippers sparkled.

This is it! Amber said to herself. The dreaded moment had arrived where she must climb the winding steps up the steep hill, enter through the wide Palace gates and cross the vast courtyard. *This is where Cinderella makes her grand entrance!*

Up the steps, wishing she was anywhere but here. Through the iron gates where the sentries raised their spears and saluted. Across the courtyard with its splashing fountain, towards the Palace with its tall battlements and huge front doors standing open, with the sound of music drifting out . . .

Oh no! Amber almost lost her nerve as she stood in the palace entrance.

Inside she could see the portraits of kings and queens on the walls and the silent marble statues in the hallway.

This is so not me! Amber thought.

Then Prince Charming and his courtiers

stepped forward to greet her.

The Prince was dressed in a long jacket of blue velvet embroidered with gold. His black leather boots came up to the knees of his tight white trousers.

"Who is this?" the Prince asked his

right-hand man as they approached their guest.

The lord looked down his list. "It can only be Cinderella," he whispered under his breath. "She is the last person to arrive."

And the Prince gazed at Amber – at her sparkling glass slippers and her flowing pink gown, at the blue velvet cloak which matched his own jacket but which glittered with diamonds like tiny stars in the night sky. And then at her perfect face, pale and round, with big, sparkling brown eyes, and her dark, dark hair where a dainty diamond tiara was set with a ruby of deepest pink.

Amber blushed under the Prince's gaze. She remembered her manners enough to

42

bow her head and drop a neat curtsey. When she looked up again, the Prince stood so close to her that he could reach out and take her hand.

"Welcome, Cinderella," he said warmly. "Welcome to my home."

Amber let Prince Charming lead her across the hall. They paraded past the statues with the Prince's lords in tow. The music grew louder as they approached the crowded ballroom.

"Who is this?" the ladies by the door whispered as they caught their first glimpse of Amber on the Prince's arm.

"I have no idea," came the answer.

44

"I've never seen her in my life before!"

"Who is her dressmaker?"

"Where did she buy that beautiful tiara – and the diamond-studded cloak – and those amazing shoes?"

The whispers grew to a loud hiss and drowned out all other talk.

"Who is this? Where has she come from? She is easily the prettiest girl here!"

Save me, someone! Amber held her breath and tugged back from view.

"Come with me," Prince Charming said, leading her gently on.

"Nonsense – she is nothing to look at!" The first voice was raised against Amber. It was shrill and loud, and belonged to a tall, skinny figure in a lilac dress.

"I agree – she is a very common girl," a

second guest agreed. Her peach pink dress clashed with her flushed complexion. The seams strained at her stout waist.

Amber swallowed hard. *Charlotte and Louisa! Trust them to rain on the parade!*

She waited in dread for them to get a proper look at her.

It was Louisa who pushed herself to the front of the gawping crowd.

"Look at her – she's much too thin!" Louisa pointed a podgy finger.

"Too fat!" Charlotte scoffed as she too shoved herself to the front.

"Awful dress!" Louisa muttered.

"Nasty, cheap tiara with fake diamonds!" Charlotte mocked.

They don't recognise me! Amber allowed herself a small smile of satisfaction.

"And those glittery shoes – eugh!" the Uglies said together.

From a balcony high above, their mother, Octavia, watched the new arrival with icy calm.

Oblivious to all this, Prince Charming led Cinderella into the centre of the vast room. "Cinderella," he said with a low bow. "Would you do me the honour of partnering me in the first dance?"

But before Amber could answer, a tall figure in a deep purple gown pushed her to one side.

"Your Highness!" the Countess of Sylvaria gushed, wafting her fan in Amber's face and giving her another hefty shove. "Shall I instruct the musicians to play the first waltz? Is it time for the dancing to begin?"

Amber staggered back into the arms of Louisa and Charlotte. They gawped down at her flushed face.

"Cinder . . .?" Charlotte stammered.

". . . ella?" Louisa gasped.

"Yes, it's me!" Amber snapped, standing up and straightening her tiara. "Keep your hands off!"

For Charlotte had reached out to snatch the tiara and Louisa was making a grab for Amber's dainty pearl necklace – a finishing touch which Fairy G must have added without Amber noticing.

"It can't be!" Louisa hissed.

"It's impossible!" Charlotte glared.

"What the matter? Didn't you think I'd scrub up this good?" Amber challenged, relieved to see that the Countess was sidetracking the Prince.

"Ah, Countess!" Prince Charming tried to live up to his name by not being rude to Cinderella's pushy rival. "I'm so pleased to see that you're enjoying yourself. Did you have a safe journey here?"

"Yes, yes," the Countess of Sylvaria assured him. Her frock was purple, her shawl was purple, so were her shoes and fan. A huge amethyst sparkled from the purple ribbon around her neck. "But the musicians, Your Highness – shall I tell them to play?"

"By all means, Countess," the Prince said with a slight bow.

"And you wait here and allow me to have the first dance with you." *Or else!*

Prince Charming cleared his throat and glanced across the room at Cinderella.

"What are you doing here?" Charlotte demanded, pinching Amber's arm.

"Why aren't you at home?" Louisa wanted to know.

"It's a long story . . . don't ask me to explain!" Amber begged.

"Madam," the Prince told the Countess, "it would of course be a pleasure to dance with you. But I have already chosen my partner for the waltz."

"Nonsense!" she replied, furrowing her brow. "I have travelled all the way from

Sylvaria. I am a countess. Of course you must have the first dance with me!"

"We'll send you packing, Cinderella!" Louisa got Amber in an armlock.

"We'll tell Mama!" Charlotte vowed.

From the balcony, steely Octavia looked down.

"Countess," Prince Charming began more firmly. "I am charmed you are here. You look wonderful – so – so young in that gown! My dear mother, the Queen, would love that style if she had been here instead of called away to visit her sister in Montatia."

"Your *mother*?" The haughty Countess went pale and deadly quiet.

"But now you must excuse me," Prince Charming said with a departing bow. "For it is time for the dancing to begin."

"Where did you get this dress?" Louisa demanded, tugging at Amber's bows.

"And this cloak?" Charlotte grabbed the velvet wrap from Amber's shoulders and flung it to the floor.

Out of the corner of her eye, Amber saw the Prince heading back towards her. Then she spotted Octavia glaring down from the balcony.

"I bet you stole them!" Louisa decided. "Yes, thief!"

"Mama will punish you, just you wait!" Charlotte threatened.

OK, Prince, you're my only escape! Amber decided. If waltzing was the only way out, waltzing was what she would do.

Prince Charming frowned at the Uglies.

But he smiled warmly at Amber and held out his hand. "Cinderella, don't be shy," he said. "I will look after you."

So Amber escaped the clutches of the Ugly Sisters and curtsied to the Prince. He bowed then led her into the centre of the dance floor.

A violinist began to play – 1-2-3, 1-2-3 – a slow, sweeping rhythm. All eyes were on the Prince and his bewitching partner.

"So sweet!" people murmured.

"So pretty!"

"So . . . perfect!"

1-2-3 – more violins joined in, then deeper stringed instruments and clarinets and oboes.

Help! Amber thought, her knees trembling. *I never waltzed in my life!*

"Step-2-3, step-2-3," Prince Charming murmured in her ear. He held her round the waist. "Ready?"

She nodded and they were off, gliding around the empty floor as Louisa, Charlotte and the Countess glowered. Prince Charming and Amber turned and swept on in time to the music.

I'm getting the hang of this! Amber said to herself, turning this way and that. Her pink satin skirt billowed out behind her, her ribbons fluttered and her glass slippers sparkled. *In fact, though I say it myself – I'm pretty good!*

"Cinderella was always such a show-off!" Louisa hissed.

"Yes, who does she think she is, the little upstart?" Charlotte frowned.

"I must put a stop to this," Octavia said out loud, though no one was listening. "And I must do it quickly!"

6

I've seen this on TV! Amber thought as Prince Charming twirled her round the dance floor. *Women in frilly frocks, men prancing around.* 1-2-3. 1-2-3. Step and twirl, step and twirl. Gradually other dancers joined them. *Actually, it's quite cool!*

"Are you having a good time?" the Prince asked, his arm still around Amber's waist.

She nodded-2-3.

"Splendid!"-2-3.

Turn and face the other way-2-3.

"Cinderella, why have we never met before?" the Prince asked. "How does a pretty girl like you manage to stay hidden away in a kingdom as small as this one?"

Cheesy! Amber thought. But here was something else that surprised her – in spite of herself she was beginning to think that His Royal Highness, Prince C was OK. Quite nice, actually.

"I don't go out much," she said. Nice not in a soppy way, but as in big-brother-who-would-look-out-for-you. And he definitely was cool looking too.

"Well I'm glad you came to the Ball." Change direction-2-3. "I'll tell you a secret

– I wasn't really looking forward to it until you showed up." -2-3.

"You weren't?"

"If I'm honest, no. Parties can be a bore unless you find someone you really want to talk to."

"They can?" *Wait until I tell Pearl and Lily that Prince Charming actually is what his name says he is!* Amber thought.

1-2-3. 1 . . . 2 . . . 3 – the music slowed. Couples twirled to a halt.

"Bravo!" Courtiers and guests cheered Prince Charming and Cinderella at the end of the first waltz.

"Sneaky little spoilsport!" Charlotte and Louisa watched from a distance, green with envy.

The Countess of Sylvaria sat in a corner in a huff.

"That was perfect," the Prince said to Amber as he led her from the floor. "Will you dance the next one with me?"

Out of breath after all that stepping and twirling, Amber nodded.

Prince Charming beamed. "Wonderful!"

But then the lord who had been carrying the guest list when Amber arrived hurried up to his prince and whispered in his ear. Prince Charming's expression changed. He frowned then whispered back. "Send word that I will come straight away," he told his courtier.

"But first I must speak with the man who brought the message. Find him and bring him to me."

The lord nodded and hurried away, while Prince Charming turned back to Amber. "I have had bad news," he said. "A messenger rode on horseback across the mountains to say that my mother, the Queen, has fallen seriously ill in Montatia."

"I'm sorry!" Amber replied. The Prince looked so worried that she reached out to squeeze his hand.

"They say she is very weak and is asking to see me. I must ride through the night to see her."

"Of course."

"But the party will go on," Prince

Charming insisted, calling for the musicians to begin the next tune. "And, Cinderella, will you promise me one thing before I go. Will you come back and visit me, here in the Palace?"

The question startled Amber, but she was sorry for the Prince and so she nodded.

"Soon?" he insisted, looking deep into her eyes.

"Soon!" she whispered, feeling bad for telling a lie.

Because, as soon as Prince Charming was out of sight, she was slap back in the middle of danger from the Uglies and their vicious Mama.

And Amber's plan of action, the moment the Prince was out of the door, was to get out of Cinderella world for good!

*

"Where is the Prince? Where did he go?" The guests were bewildered as the musicians struck up a fast, skipping polka.

"There was an urgent message," someone said. "His Highness had to rush away."

"But the party will go on!" The Countess of Sylvaria sprang up from her chair and grabbed the nearest spare duke. "The Prince has commanded it. Come, everyone – join the dance!"

Amber watched a few of the guests hop half-heartedly around the room. A party without the Prince just wasn't the same.

I'm out of here! she thought, heading for the nearest exit.

"Oh no you don't!" Tall Charlotte

blocked Amber's way like a goalkeeper in front of goal.

"Come back, you sneak!" Louisa yelled, rugby tackling from behind.

But Amber was nippier than either of the Uglies. She darted sideways and spotted a French window opening out on to an inner courtyard. She was through it before Louisa and Charlotte could gather their wits.

Better! Amber breathed in the fresh night air. She looked up at the stars and round the courtyard at a dozen different doors she could choose for her great escape.

Behind her, in the crowded ballroom, the Uglies collided and screeched insults.

"Get up off the floor, slowcoach!" Charlotte yelled at her dumpy sister.

"Why didn't you grab her, you useless beanpole?" Louisa shrieked.

Good riddance, Amber thought, choosing the nearest door. *By the time they've finished arguing, I'll be far away!*

The heavy door led to a long corridor lined with portraits of people and horses. There were rusty swords hanging on hooks and shiny hunting bugles.

Where does this lead? Amber wondered, but Louisa and Charlotte's voices grew louder as they burst out into the courtyard in hot pursuit. She had no time to stop and think.

So she picked up her long skirts and ran to the end of the gloomy corridor, convinced that the eyes in the portraits followed her progress, afraid that the heavy swords would crash down from their hooks.

Spooky! she said to herself, wrenching at the handle of the door that blocked her exit. *If I was Prince Charming, I'd give this place a makeover and have it brightened up a bit!*

Wrenching hard, Amber managed to turn the handle. The hinges creaked as she pushed the door open.

Yuck! She stepped straight into a filmy cobweb. The way ahead was too dark to see. Yet Amber knew that if she turned back, she might run into the Uglies again. *Get a grip!* she told herself. *Keep going straight ahead. In the end, this is bound to come out somewhere safe!*

So she edged forward in her glass

slippers and party frock, brushing aside more cobwebs and feeling her way with her fingertips along the rough wall.

At last she stumbled against some stone steps leading down to a low doorway. She fumbled in the dark for a handle, turned it and pushed hard.

This door creaked worse than the last, but at least there was light in the next corridor, from flaming torches slotted into rusty brackets on the walls.

Better! Amber thought with relief. Now at least she could see where she was going.

But which way should she choose? Tiptoeing up and down, she saw there were no windows in the corridor, only low stone arches leading in many different directions, all gloomy and dimly lit.

More spiders! she shuddered. *And it doesn't smell good down here either. Guess what – I think I'm in the dungeons!*

Amber realised that her escape wasn't going as well as she'd hoped. "It's no good – I'll have to turn around and go back the way I came," she muttered out loud. "Now which door did I come through? This one? No, this one. That one?"

Each door she tried was locked, until at last she found the right one.

Up the steps into the musty, pitch black corridor. Portraits peering down from the wall. Swords hanging from frayed ropes . . .

Swish! A gleaming blade swung in front of Amber's eyes. It was held in a hand with tapered fingers that wore an emerald ring which glinted in the low light of a guttering candle. The hand belonged to a long, slim arm, the arm to an elegant shoulder and neck . . . the neck to a cruel, white, mask-like face topped with a high, powdered wig.

"Octavia!" Amber gasped.

7

"Help! Help!" Amber cried in terror.

Octavia advanced, sword in hand. "Now, once and for all, I will be rid of you!" she vowed.

Amber backed against the wall. "Help!" she wailed.

"Save your breath. Who will hear you?" Octavia sneered, advancing with the sword. "These walls are thick. No one

knows that we are here."

"You're a wicked woman!" Amber whimpered. Then she had to clench her teeth to stop them from chattering.

"And you, Cinderella, are a simpleton – a little fool!" Octavia told her. "You think you are clever to fulfil your ambition of escaping from my cellar and dancing with the Prince. But I will not be defied!"

"I'll tell you one thing," Amber shot back. "Louisa and Charlotte stand no chance with Prince Charming, if that's what all this is about. Even if you get rid of me, he won't look at them, not in a million years!"

Enraged, Octavia raised the sword above her head. "I'll stop your nonsense for good, you insolent girl!"

Amber cowered in the corner, dreading the next move.

But there was no flash of steel as the sword descended. Instead, there were loud footsteps charging down the corridor and a terrific yell of "Run, Cinders!" as a slight figure threw itself full tilt at Octavia and brought her crashing down.

"Run!" Buttons told Amber again. He lifted a picture from the wall and smashed it over the wicked enemy's head. She sprawled, dazed and confused, on the floor.

"Don't even ask!" Buttons winked at Amber.

Octavia lay groaning, her head poking through the torn canvas, her tiara crooked over one eye.

"How did you . . . when did you . . . why did you . . .?" Amber stammered. She could hardly breathe from the shock of it all.

"I said, don't ask, Cinders." Buttons straightened his jacket and tugged at his cuffs. "Ask no questions, be told no lies."

"You followed me here," Amber realised. "You've been watching every move I made!"

"Someone has to keep an eye on you," he pointed out. "I knew Octavia wouldn't be happy when you turned up out of the blue."

"Uuh-uuh-uh!" Octavia groaned.

"Come on, let's get out of here," Buttons decided. He led the way back along the corridor and Amber followed. When they reached the door leading out into the courtyard, they turned to make sure that Octavia wasn't hot on their heels.

"I reckon she's still groggy from that whack on the head," Amber told him.

"No more than she deserved," he replied, dragging Amber through the door and bolting it firmly from the outside. "And now she's not going anywhere!" he added with a grin.

"Except the dungeons!" Amber grinned back.

"Leave her with the spiders and creepy crawlies, where she belongs!" Buttons dusted his hands together to show a job well done. "Now, Cinders, do you think you can get by without me?"

"What do you mean?" She glanced round the courtyard at the stone statues and neat, clipped bushes. In the ballroom the music still played.

"I mean, can you make it through the rest of the evening without getting into any more trouble?"

"Course I can," Amber tutted. "Why? Does that mean you still won't join the party?"

Buttons nodded. "You know me, Cinders. I prefer a good old knees-up back home with my gran."

Amber nodded. She remembered the kind old lady sitting in her chair by the fire, asking her to dance round the cosy attic room. "Say hi to your gran from me," she said quietly.

He backed away, smiling and nodding.

"You could still come!" she insisted, pointing towards the ballroom.

"Another time, Cinders," Buttons said a touch sadly.

Something came over her – a sudden rush to the head as she realised this was goodbye for good. She darted forward to hug him. "I'm going to miss you, Buttons."

"Whoa!" he cried, struggling free. "Steady on."

She smiled and stood back. "Goodbye," she said softly.

"Ta-ta!" Buttons said, sticking his hands

in his pockets and strolling off without looking back. "'And this little piggy cried wee-wee-wee-wee,'" he sang, "'All the way home!'"

8

"All is well!" Prince Charming announced to his guests as Amber rejoined the party. "I spoke to the messenger who soon confessed that the news from Montatia was false. My mother is in good health after all!"

"How peculiar!" The Countess of Sylvaria was the first to speak. "Why would anyone wish to alarm you in that way?"

"Someone who wanted to spoil our celebrations," the Prince declared. "The guilty messenger will give us the name of that person, all in good time."

I bet I know it already! Amber thought with a frown. She pictured Octavia, her head framed by torn canvas, left with a bad headache, groaning in the dark. This fake message showed all the signs of being one of Octavia's cunning schemes, to separate Cinderella from the Prince and create a chance to nab her.

"But they did not succeed, thank goodness." Prince Charming spied Amber across the room and strode towards her. "For now I can dance once more with the girl of my dreams!"

"Hush!" Amber murmured as she

blushed deeply. "Don't say that!"

"Why not? It is true!" the gallant Prince said.

"Simpering idiot!" Charlotte muttered under her breath as she and Louisa watched from the sidelines.

"Yes, Cinderella is such a simpleton!" Louisa agreed.

"Not her – *him!*" Charlotte shot back, her beady eye fixed on Prince Charming. "Keep up, Louisa! Prince Charming is a deluded fool if he imagines Cinderella is the girl of his dreams."

"He'll judge differently when he discovers she is nothing but a wretched kitchen girl!" Louisa agreed in a loud voice.

"Hush!" their neighbours warned as the

musicians struck up another waltz.

"Whoever saw two such prune-faced spoilsports?" they whispered between themselves.

This time Amber didn't need her partner to show her the steps. As the Prince held her waist, she glided into the dance and let the music take her whirling around the grand ballroom, under a thousand glittering drops of crystal chandelier, past smiling faces and fluttering fans, between swirling silks and sparkling jewels. Round and round she danced.

"Are you happy, Cinderella?" the Prince asked.

She nodded. Actually yes, she was. Dance-dance-dancing in the arms of a handsome prince!

The night went on. The Countess of Sylvaria waltzed with her duke, all the young ladies found perfect partners, even Louisa and Charlotte dragged doddery old men from their chairs to join a polka.

"Where's Mama?" Louisa hissed at Charlotte as they propped up their partners and staggered by.

"No idea!" Charlotte replied airily. Her rickety old man was a *Sir* Somebody and so she was happy.

Prince Charming danced and danced with his Cinderella. He wouldn't let her catch her breath until at last a lord came up at the end of a galloping gavotte and whispered in his ear. Then the Prince clapped his hands for attention. "Time for the fireworks to begin!" he cried.

He called for Amber's velvet cloak and led her out of the ballroom into the front courtyard. All the party guests followed, chattering and breathless.

"Ooh!" they cried when the first rockets

showered red, green and gold fountains from the night sky.

"Ah!" Firecrackers crackled, silver Catherine wheels whizzled and whirled over the Palace.

Amber gazed up at the magic sight of golden rain and shooting stars. Prince Charming stood happily by her side.

There were more cries of delight, much applause amid the loud bangs and crackles of the fireworks.

One – two – three! The clock in the town square began to chime midnight.

That was pretty! Amber thought as a row of red and green Roman candles flared and lit up the faces of a thousand spectators.

Four – five – six!

Wow! Amber gazed up at a million spluttering golden sparks. But what was that other noise from down in the town? Was it the chiming of the big clock? *Seven – eight – nine.* Yes, it was striking midnight!

Amber gasped and spun around. Midnight! How could she have forgotten Fairy G's warning? She left Prince

Charming without a word and pressed through the crowd, hurrying as fast as she could.

"Ooh – aaah!" The crowd loved the silver shooting stars best of all.

"Would you believe it – I almost left it too late!" Amber cried out loud as she reached the Palace gate and looked down the long flight of stone steps leading to the town. "I never even heard the clock begin to strike!"

"Cinderella, come back!"

Amber heard Prince Charming shout her name. Frantically she set off down the steps to the sound of fireworks whooshing and crackling overhead.

Ten – eleven – twelve. Midnight!

In her haste, Amber lost a glass slipper.

It fell from her foot as she raced into the darkness of the town. It glittered and sparkled on the step for her prince to find.

9

Amber was back in her old rags. She'd felt the pink satin gown change into a worn and ragged red skirt, her blue velvet cloak into a plain woollen shawl. On her hat was a battered straw hat in place of her glittering diamond and ruby tiara.

"Oh!" she cried, as she wandered helplessly through the town square. She wept bitterly for her lost fairy-tale world.

It's so not fair! she thought, hanging her head and shedding real tears. *One minute I'm the happiest girl in the world, the next I'm the most wretched!*

"It's over," she murmured sadly. "The clock struck twelve. I lost everything."

On she went through the empty streets and down alleyways, while on the hill above there was the sound of laughter and music. The last fireworks exploded in the sky.

"What's left for me now?" Amber said to a stray black cat. "Only a dark cellar and a dying fire."

Slowly she made her way back to the house. The hard cobbles hurt her bare feet, she felt wearier than she had ever felt before.

"Huh, you're back, I see." Tom the footman spotted her as she trudged home. He held the door open with a mock bow. "Your grand jaunt in the golden coach didn't last long. Now it's back to earth with a bump!"

Amber turned her head and ignored him. She tiptoed down the hallway, hoping that upstairs the old man would be fast asleep.

But the click of the closing door must have disturbed him. "Cinderella, is that you?" a querulous voice asked.

Amber ducked out of sight. "Yes, Papa, it's me," she called back.

"And did you have a lovely time?"

"Yes, thank you, Pa, I did!"

"Good. Now go to bed and sleep well,"

he said kindly as he closed his door.

Amber sighed and went on, down into the cellar. Tears dripped from the tip of her nose as she sat down beside the ashes of the fire.

Whoosh! Her fairy godmother gave her no time to sit and mope. She appeared in a twinkle of silver dust.

"Tut-tut, Cinderella, you did not heed my advice," she began.

Miserably Amber shook her head.

"You were told to leave before the clock struck midnight," Fairy G reminded her. "And what do you do? Why, you dance with the Prince and you forget every word I said!"

"I didn't . . . it wasn't like that," Amber tried to explain.

The fairy held up her hand. "Now, Cinderella, don't waste your breath. I know precisely what went on and I know I'm right. You were so dizzy with happiness that you forgot to leave until it was too late. Now look at you!"

"Yeah, I'm a mess," Amber admitted, gathering her rags about her. She felt like the naughty kid hauled up in front of the head teacher.

"Tut-tut," Fairy G said again. "I have to say, Cinderella, that I'm extremely disappointed in you. I expected better."

"I'm sorry," Amber mumbled, hanging her head and wishing it was over.

"You let me down."

"I didn't mean to – a lot happened that you don't know about."

Amber sighed. She knew it was time to say goodbye to all this – to Octavia and the Uglies, to Prince Charming. And with tears in her eyes, goodbye to Buttons.

The fairy fluttered her wings and gazed sadly at Amber. "Hmm. Perhaps I can bring back your beautiful ball gown. Let's see."

Quickly Fairy G waved her wand. A

cloud of silver light surrounded Amber.

Whoosh! She looked down and saw that she was back in her satin gown and diamond tiara.

But now the fairy fiddled with her wand and sighed loudly. "I'm afraid that's all I can do," she told Amber. "I have run out of magic for you, my dear."

"That's OK!" Amber said quickly. She took a last look around the cellar. "Goodbye!" she whispered. Then she closed her eyes.

And she thought very hard about her basement at home, about her dressing-up box, and Lily and Pearl waiting for her there.

10

Whoosh!

"She didn't even have to wave her wand!" Amber-Cinderella told Lily and Pearl.

Lily rubbed her eyes. Pearl stood with her mouth open.

They'd seen the gold and silver mist thing and heard the *whoosh*. Then Amber had reappeared in full Cinderella gear.

"I'm talking about my fairy godmother – she didn't have to do any actual magic!"

"*Your* fairy godmother?" Lily echoed.

Amber watched the sparkly glitter settle around her dainty glass slipper. She grinned and wiggled her toes when she saw that the other foot was bare.

"You're telling us she has a wand that does real magic?" Pearl gasped.

"That's what I've been trying to tell you all along, only you wouldn't believe me!" Amber insisted. Here she was, back in her own basement, dressed like a fairy-tale princess. How cool was that!

"We believe you now," Lily assured her. "This is the fourth time you've popped off in a cloud of glitter and whooshed back again."

"All dressed up like Cinderella," Pearl muttered, staring at Amber's beautiful pink satin gown and glittering tiara. "Are those real diamonds?" she asked.

Amber gave a little smile but said nothing.

"You lost a shoe," Lily pointed out.

Amber nodded. "This *is* Cinderella we're talking about, remember!"

Lily and Pearl tiptoed round her, studying her from head to foot. "So did you get to marry Prince Charming?" Lily asked.

"Course not." Amber laughed at the very idea. "Though he would've asked me if I'd stuck around. Anyway, do you want me to give you a twirl?"

"No!" Pearl and Lily begged. "Stand

still, Amber. Don't move. We don't want you vanishing on us again!"

"Don't worry, I won't," Amber agreed, slipping her hands inside her warm cloak and finding a hidden pocket, where she felt a flat, round object. Puzzled, she pulled it out.

"What's that?" Pearl asked.

"Don't ask me." Amber showed Pearl and Lily a small silver mirror studded with rubies. It had a carved handle and was the sort of mirror meant for fancy dressing-tables in ladies' bedrooms.

"Mirror, mirror, on the wall!" Lily laughed. "Where did it come from, Amber?"

Amber-Cinderella shrugged. "I've never seen it before."

Lily took it from her and turned it over

and over in her hand.

"Come on, you two, I'm bored with this. Let's play something else!" Pearl cried, stuffing clothes back into the dressing-up box.

But Lily wouldn't let go of the mirror. Instead she slipped it into her own pocket then went outside with the others to play.

Have you checked out...

www.dressingupdreams.net

It's the place to go for games, downloads, activities, sneak previews and lots of fun!

You'll find a special dressing-up game and lots of activities and fun things to do, as well as news on Dressing-Up Dreams and all your favourite characters.

Sign up to the newsletter at **www.dressingupdreams.net** to receive extra clothes for your Dressing-Up Dreams doll and the opportunity to enter special members only competitions.

What happens next...?
Log onto www.dressingupdreams.net
for a sneak preview of my next adventure!

WIN A Dressing-Up Dreams GOODIE BAG!

CAN YOU SPOT THE TWO DIFFERENCES AND THE HIDDEN LETTER IN THESE TWO PICTURES OF AMBER?

There is a spot-the-difference picture and hidden letter in the back of all four Dressing-Up Dreams books about Amber (look for the books with to 4 on the spine). Hidden in one of the pictures above is a secret letter. Find all four letters and put them together to make a special Dressing-Up Dreams word, then send it to us. Each month, we will put the correct entries in a draw and one lucky winner will receive a magical Dressing-Up Dreams goodie bag including an exclusive Dressing-Up Dreams keyring!

Send your magical word, your name and your address
on a postcard to: **The Dressing-Up Dreams Competition**

UK Readers:	**Australian Readers:**	**New Zealand Readers:**
Hodder Children's Books	Hachette Children's Books	Hachette Livre NZ Ltd
338 Euston Road	Level 17/207 Kent Street	PO Box 100 749
London NW1 3BH	Sydney NSW 2000	North Shore City 0745
hsmarketing@hodder.co.uk	childrens.books@hachette.com.au	childrensbooks@hachette.co.nz

Only one entry per child. Final draw: 27th February 2009
For full terms and conditions go to www.hachettechildrens.co.uk/terms

COLOURING FUN!

Carefully colour the Dressing-Up Dreams picture on the next page and then send it in to us.

Or you can draw your very own fairytale character. You might want to think about what they would wear or if they have special powers.

Each month, we will put the best entries on the website gallery and one lucky winner will receive a magical Dressing-Up Dreams goodie bag!

Send your drawing, your name and your address on a postcard to:
The Dressing-Up Dreams Competition

UK Readers:
Hodder Children's Books
338 Euston Road
London NW1 3BH
kidsmarketing@hodder.co.uk

Australian Readers:
Hachette Children's Books
Level 17/207 Kent Street
Sydney NSW 2000
childrens.books@hachette.com.au

New Zealand Readers:
Hachette Livre NZ Ltd
PO Box 100 749
North Shore City 0745
childrensbooks@hachette.co

For full terms and conditions go to www.hachettechildrens.co.uk/terms